Thomas Rogers

Celestiall Elegies of The Goddesses and the Muses

deploring the death of the Right Honourable and vertuous Ladie the Ladie

Fravnces Countesse of Hertford

.

Thomas Rogers

Celestiall Elegies of The Goddesses and the Muses
deploring the death of the Right Honourable and vertuous Ladie the Ladie Fravnces Countesse of Hertford

ISBN/EAN: 9783337196400

Printed in Europe, USA, Canada, Australia, Japan

Cover: Foto ©Andreas Hilbeck / pixelio.de

More available books at **www.hansebooks.com**

CELESTIALL ELEGIES.

ROGERS'S CELESTIALL ELEGIES.

THIS poetical Tract, like the others in the volume, is printed from an unique exemplar. Not only is no other copy known, but apparently no mention has been made of it by any Bibliographer or Biographer. . It is marked by more ability and intereſt than the one which follows.

The author was poſſibly the ſame Thomas Rogers, a native of Glouceſterſhire (being born in or near to Tewkeſbury), who lived moſtly, in his latter days, in the pariſh of St. Giles in the Fields, London, and who publiſhed, in 1612, a funeral tribute to the memory of Prince Henry under the quaint (perhaps intended as a punning) title of " Glouceſters Myte." Dr. Bliſs, who, in his edition of Wood's " Athenæ Oxonienſes," gives the concluding ſtanza of it, mentions a copy as being in the Bodleian Library, but it is not known to exiſt elſewhere.

Some intereſting alluſions will be found ſcattered through the work. Among them may be noticed the following :—In Quatorzain 8, Bajazeth and Tamberlaine. [Marlowe's play on this ſubjeſt was printed in 1590.] In Quatorzain 12, "Seas of troubles ;" and "aſting a part upon this worldly ſtage ". [The firſt alluſion here is curious, for Shakeſpeare's play of "Hamlet", in which it occurs, is fuppofed not to have been written before 1602-3]. In Quatorzain 13, a poor attempt at a pun. In Quatorzain 14, fome far-fetched Similes. In Quatorzain 14, allufions to " Thetis ftreames ", and " the rockes by Netleys fhores ", etc.

The " Ladie Fraunces, Counteffe of Hertford," here commemorated, was the third daughter of Lord William Howard, firft Lord Howard of Effingham (created Lord Admiral by Queen Mary), by his fecond wife, Margaret, fecond daughter of Sir Thomas Gamage, and fifter of Charles, fecond Lord Howard of Effingham, who was created Earl of Nottingham in 1596. The latter was the chivalrous Lord High Admiral of England who did fuch good fervice againft the Spanifh Armada in 1588, as well as on other occafions. His firft wife was the Lady Katharine Cary, daughter of Henry Cary, Lord Hunfdon, and the fubject of the following poetical tribute by Thomas Powell : confequently the two ladies were fifters-in-law.

The Countefs of Hertford died without iffue 14 May, 1598, aged 44, and was buried in the Chapel of St. Benedict, Weftminfter Abbey; againft the eaft wall of which Chapel is a magnificent monument, twenty-eight feet high, with a fuitable infcription to her memory.

" This monument occupies the place of the original altar, and was probably erected within two years after the Counteff's demife, when the two fteps to the altar were made to ferve as basements to it. This ftately tomb is enriched with columns and pyramids of various kinds of marble, decorated with the enfigns and devices of the noble families of Somerfet and Effingham. The Countefs is reprefented in her robes, in a recumbent pofture, with her head refting on an embroidered cufhion, and her feet on a lion's back." Abridged from *Ackermann's Hiftory of Weftminfter Abbey*, vol. 2. p. 109.

Traces of the gold on the embroidery of the cufhion and of the crimfon colour on the robes may ftill be observed.

This lady's eldeft fifter was named Douglas, and her career was an extraordinary one. She was married, firft, to John Lord Sheffield ;

fecondly to Robert Dudley, Earl of Leicefter; and thirdly, to Sir Edward Stafford. An account of her intrigues with Leicefter (during her firft hufband's life), will be found in Gervafe Holles's curious Memoirs of the Holles family. Her marriage with Lord Leicefter, however, was denied by him ; and in confequence, her fon, the celebrated Sir Robert Dudley, was declared illegitimate.

The principal events in the life of the Earl of Hertford are too eafily acceffible to require a lengthened notice here. Suffice it to fay, that, though the malice of the enemies of his father, the Protector Somerfet, deprived him, after the fall of that great nobleman, of his hereditary dignities and eftates, the favour of Queen Elizabeth, immediately on her acceffion, in November, 1558, reftored them to him. But his firft marriage, very early in life, with Lady Catherine Grey (the fifter of Lady Jane Grey), who had certain claims to the Succeffion, provoked the ire of his fovereign to fuch an extent, that he was not only fined by the Star Chamber in the fum of £15,000, but was, with his unfortunate wife, committed to the Tower. After a captivity of four years fhe was releafed, but never faw her hufband again. She died 26 January, 1567-8. The Earl was not releafed till he had fuffered nine years' imprifonment. The fate of their grandfon, Sir William Seymour, was fomewhat fimilar, for having married the Lady Arabella Stuart, her nearnefs to the throne excited the jealoufy and apprehenfions of the reigning fovereign, and led to her imprifonment, lunacy, and early death.

The Earl's fecond wife was the Lady Frances Howard—the fubject of the following poetical tribute—who died in 1598, and by whom he had no iffue.

His third wife, whom he married when he was upwards of fixty years old, was alfo of noble defcent, and her character may be given in the words of Granger (*Biographical Hiftory of England*). "She was Frances, daughter to Thomas, Lord Howard of Bindon, fon to Thomas, Duke of Norfolk. She was firft married to one Prannel, a vintner's fon in London, who was poſſeſſed of a good eſtate. This match ſeems to have been the effeҫt of youthful paſſion. Upon the deceaſe of Prannel, who lived but a ſhort time after his marriage [he died in December, 1599], ſhe was courted by Sir George Rodney, a weſt-country gentleman, to whoſe addreſſes ſhe ſeemed to liſten ; but ſoon deſerted him, and was married to Edward, Earl of Hertford [about 27 May, 1601]. Upon his marriage, Sir George wrote her a tender copy of verſes in his own blood, and preſently after ran himſelf upon his ſword. Her third huſband was Lodowick, Duke of Richmond and Lenox, who left her [in February 1623-4], a very amiable widow. The aims of great beauties, like thoſe of conquerors, are boundleſs. Upon the death of the Duke, ſhe aſpired to the King, but died in her ſtate of widowhood [8th Oҫtober, 1639, aged 63; leaving no children.] " " Her will, dated 28th July, and proved 31st Oҫtober, 1639, is" (says Col. Cheſter in his valuable ' Marriage, Baptiſmal, and Burial Regiſters of Weſtminſter Abbey 1875') "very long and of marvellous hiſtorical and genealogical intereſt, and contains one eccentric direҫtion (for a lady of her years), viz: that her body ſhall not be opened, but packed in bran before it is cold, and buried wrapt in thoſe ſheets wherein my lord and I firſt ſlept that night when we were married."

She lies buried in Weſtminſter Abbey, in the ſame grave with her third huſband—who, like herſelf and her ſecond huſband, had been three times married. The ſplendid monument which covers their remains, and which was ereҫted by her, is thus deſcribed in Ackermann's work on that edifice.

" This tomb, which is of braſs, almoſt fills the chapel to the north of Henry the Seventh's monument. The figures of the Duke and Ducheſs are finely caſt; but the caryatides, which ſupport a canopy of various ornamental pierced ſcroll-work, in the charaҫters of Faith, Hope, Charity, and Prudence, poſſeſs ſuperior excellence. The figure of Fame, on the top, is repreſented in the aҫt of taking her flight; and the urns are copied after antique forms."

A curious account of this beautiful, attractive, and eccentric lady will be found in Arthur Wilſon's Life and Reign of K. James I. publiſhed in 1653, folio. Lodge, however, in his " Portraits of Illuſtrious Perſonages of Great Britain," has inſerted a leſs prejudiced life of the Ducheſs, to accompany her portrait, which is there engraved after a full-length picture by Vandyck, dated 1633, in the poſſeſſion of the Marquis of Bath. Another engraved portrait of her by William Pas, dated 1623, after a painting by Van Somer, formerly poſſeſſed by Horace Walpole at Strawberry Hill, is prefixed to ſome preſentation copies of Captain John Smith's Hiſtory of Virginia, folio, 1624, a work dedicated to the Ducheſs.

A full length portrait of the Duke of Richmond, painted by Van Somer, dated 1623, aged 59, is in the poſſeſſion of Her Majeſty at Hampton Court.

The Earl of Hertford makes no figure in the politics of his time, but towards the end of the reign of Elizabeth he muſt have regained ſome portion of her favour, as we find that in September 1591 ſhe viſited him at his ſeat of Elvetham in Hampſhire, where very elaborate entertainments, which occupied four days in repreſentation and elicited her warm approval, were given in her honour. The account of theſe feſtivities is reprinted in Nichols's Progreſſes of Q. Elizabeth vol. iii. He was alſo one of the patrons of the Stage, for in 1592, according to the Privy Council Regiſters, he had among his ſervants a body of players ; who have, however, left few materials for the hiſtorian of the drama ; differing, in this reſpect, from the comedians under the protection of his brother-in-law, the Lord Admiral, who had connected with them in their management and concerns Philip Henſlowe and Edward Alleyn. By James I. he was ſelected (in 1605) as one of the Ambaſſadors to the Archduke, an office which he accepted after much importunity, but which, in ſplendour at leaſt, did not ſuffer at his hands, for Sir Dudley Carleton, writing to Mr. Winwood, ſays, " Our great Ambaſſadors draw near their time, and you may think all will be in the beſt manner, when the little Lord Hartford makes a rate of expence of £10,000, beſides the King's allowance."

The Earl of Hertford died in April 1621, at the advanced age of 83, and is buried with his unfortunate firſt wife in Saliſbury Cathedral, in the ſouth choir-aiſle, under a ſtately though taſteleſs monument. "It is worth while", (ſays Hallam, in his *Conſtitutional Hiſtory*, in which he diſcuſſes the claims of the Counteſs to the throne) "to read the epitaph on his monument; an affecting teſtimony to the purity and faithfulneſs of an attachment rendered ſtill more ſacred by misfortune and time. Quo deſiderio veteres revocavit amores."

Of Matthew Ewens, with whom the author of the preſent tract claims relationſhip, the following account is given in Foſs's *Judges of England*. "He was called upon to take the degree of ſerjeant by writ dated 29 November, 1593, the return of which was probably in the following Hilary term. During that term, on 1 February, 1594, he was raiſed to the bench of the Exchequer; and his judgments in that and the following years are reported by Savile and Coke. Beyond this no account appears of him; but his death or reſignation ſoon after occurred, as his ſucceſſor, John Savile, was appointed in July 1598."

CELESTIALL ELEGIES

of the Goddesses and the Muses, de-
deploring *the death of the right honourable and vertuous*
Ladie the Ladie FRAVNCES Countesse of Hertford,
late wife vnto the right honorable EDVVARD
SEYMOR Vicount Beauchamp
and Earle of Hertford.

WHEREVNTO ARE ANNEXED

some funerall verses touching the death of
MATHEVV EVVENS Esquire, late one
of the Barons of her Maiesties Court of Exchequer, vnto whose the author
hereof was allyed.

Propertius Eleg. 5. Lib. 3.
Haud vllas portabis opes Acheronta ad vndas
Nudus ad infernas stulte veliere rates.

Hor. Lib. 1. Ep. ad Quint.
Mors vltima linea rerum est.

By *Thomas Rogers* Esquire.

Imprinted at London by *Richard Bradocke*, for
I. B. *and are to be sold at her shop in Paules*
Church-yard at the signe of the Bible.
1 5 9 8.

To the Right

Honourable his singuler good Lord;
the Lord Edward Seymor viscount
Beauchampe Earle of Hertford.

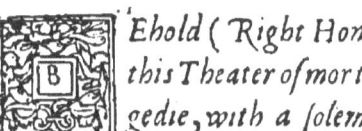Ehold (Right Honourable) in
this Theater of mortalitie a Tra-
gedie, with a solemne funerall,
at which the Goddesses are chiefe mourners,
and the Muses attendants, wherein death
plaies the Tyrannicall King or the kinglie
Tyrant, your deare Ladie and wife the sub-
iect of his furie, which in a dumbe showe is
heere presented by me: whereof I desire your

Lordſhippe to be a ſpectator and a Iudge
If I haue wittilie plaide the fooles part in
contriuing the matter (I thinke I haue plaid
the wiſeſt part :) And then I hope I ſhall
haue your Lordſhips applauſe. And that is
all I expect.

Your Lordſhips euer at
commaund.

T. R.

Celeſtiall Eligies for the late death of
the right Honourable the Ladie Fraunces
Counteſſe of Hertforde.

QVATORZAIN. 1
Berecynthia.

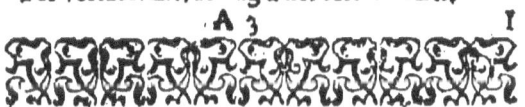

(To wes,

DRawne In my Royall chariot , crownd with
Through all the kingdoms of the centred earth,
With a great Traine of the celoſtiall Powres
That from my wombe tooke their immortall birth,
Deſcend I as chiefe mourner from the skye,
To ſolemnize this Counteſſe funerall ,
And crowne her fame with immortalitie,
Although her bodie now to death be thrall
My daughter *Cynthia* whilome lou'd her deare,
Noble ſhe was by vertue, birth, and match,
Match'd with a Peare, yet matchles without Peare.
For Pearcles ſhe, did others ouer match,
   Wherefore the Fates growne enuious of her praiſe
   For vertues ſake, ab idg'd her earthlie daies.

A 3   I

QVATORZAIN. 2.

Iuno.

I that am both *Ioues* sister and his wife,
The Queene of heauen, whom Gods & men adore
Hearing the fame of this braue Ladies life,
In mournfull habit now her death deplores
She hath putt of all earthly ornaments
And cloth'd her soule in glories spotlesse robe,
She hath exchang'd these mixed Elements,
For that pure Quintessence, the heauenlie globe
Loe how her spright infranchised from thrall,
Of sinfull flesh, ascends the Christall skye,
Scorning to dwell long in this earthly vale,
Where all men rise to fall, and liue to die:
        Therefore she soard aboue a humane pitch,
        And with her vertues doth my Realme inrich.
                                        Th

QVATORZAIN. 3.
Pallas.

THe pompe of this vaine world she did despise,
  Weighing the slipperie state of earthly things,
Therefore aboue the Spheares of heauen she flies,
To sing and ioy before the King of Kings:
Her vertues that did militate on earth,
Against the flesh, the deuill, sinne and hell,
Now triumphe in the heauens, and conquer death
And in *Ioues* holy monarchie doe dwell.
I rue the losse of true Nobilitie
Whilome inuested in her noble breast,
Wisedome with honour link't in amitie,
VVere both in her, and she in death supprest:
  How can I chuse but waile for her decease,
  Sith by her death my kingdom doth decreale.

A 4   Ay

QVATORZAIN. 4
Diana.

AY me; my vestall flame is now exrinct,
My flowre of *Chastitie* doth fade away
In *Lethes* Houds true noblenes doth sinke,
My Empyre runnes to ruinous decay;
Pittie, Almes-deeds and charitie is fled,
Fidelitie beyond the seas is gone,
True friendship now and faithfull loue is dead,
And *Priapus* vsurpeth *Cupids* throne :
She that did seeke my kingdome to maintaine,
By sanctitie, religion, faith, and zeale,
Through enuie of the Destenies is slaine,
Death robs th'Eschequer of my common weale,
For all those rites which I was wont to haue,
Are fled to heauen or buried in her graue.

IP

QVATORZAIN. 51
Venus.

IF that I am a ſtarre, Ile looſe my light ,
And fall from Heauen, vpon the earth to morne,
Becauſe her lifes faire day is turndé to night,
My ioye to griefe, my loue to hate ſhall turne.
If that I am a Goddeſſe as men ſay,
Whom louers tearme Celeſtiall and deuine,
With humaine teares Ile waſh my ioyes away,
And on the earth no more by day-time ſhine:
If I be beauties Soueraigne, and loues Queene,
Ile put a maſke of clouds before my face,
Hating to loue , louing to liue vnſeene,
I will obſcure my ſelfe in ſome darke place:
    And if I be a Planet, while I raigne,
    Ile frown on th'earth where my delight is ſlaine.
                                              From

QVATORZAIN. 6.
Thetis.

FRom th'vnknowne kingdome of th' Antipodes,
And from the fartheſt bonds of th'Ocean maine,
Attended with troopes of *Nereides*,
And charming *Syrens*, that ſupporte my traine:
Mou'd with the gentle murmure of the ſtreames,
That ſeememt humane miſeries to weepe,
I that doe kiſſe the Sunnes tranſplendent beames,
When he in *Neptunes* boſome falls a ſleepe;
Come to this famous land in waues of woe,
Like to a Queene in mourning weedes araide,
Crowned with cares, becauſe mans mortall foe,
The Tyrant death, his tragick part hath plaide;
    Seamore lamentes tnan all the worlde beſide,
    His true loues loſſe that late in England dyde.
                   My

QVATORZAIN. 7
Ceres.

MY wealth decaies for want of Somers heat,
Somers heat fades because the Sunne is fled,
The Sunne is fled, because his griefe is great,
His griefe is great, because his ioye is dead,
His ioye is dead, since his deare ladie dyde,
And since his lady dide he euer mournde,
He euer mournde, for losse of Natures pride,
For Natures pride, is now to ashes turnde,
To ashes turnde that was a *Phœnix* rare,
A *Phœnix* rare, of whom no other bred,
No other bred, that breedes the more my care,
The more my care, sith all in her is dead:
　　O Heaues, why do you bring this land such dearth,
　　As for to take a *Phœnix* from the earth.

1

QVATORZAIN. 8.

Fortuna.

I that do turne the rowling wheele of chaunce,
The blinde light Goddesse of vnconstancie,
That sometime did the Romaine Peers aduance,
To sway the worlds imperiall Monarchie:
I that doe kings enthrone, annoynt, and crowne,
And ofte depose them from the Royall seate,
I that on mightie *Baiazeth* did frowne,
And made the baseborne *Tamberlaine* so great:
Lament that death hath got the victorie,
While I am faine to flie away for feare,
For where death raines, there ends my soueraintie,
He casts downe *Trophees* which I did vpreare,
  This Ladie whome I raisde to high degree,
  Dyde not by chaunce but fatall destenie,

Red

QVATORZAIN. 9.
Nemesis.

REd hote with rage whose heart with griefe doth
I come from *Ioue* fell *Atropos* to chide, (bleede,
That cut too soone this Countesse vitall threede,
Wherewith her soule and bodie were fast tide:
While wicked men long liue in Ioy and pleasure,
She liu'd long time in sicknesse and in paine,
Who still accounted vertue her chiefe treasure,
And losse of worldly wealth heauens richest gaine:
Wherefore she fled to heauen,from whence I came,
And with reuenge to scourge mens insolence,
And those same ruthlesse destenies to tame,
That by this Ladies death *Ioues* wrath incence,
   Who let the wicked long time liue in pride,
   While she that best deserued,soonest dide.

Though

QVATORZAIN, 10.
Bellona.

THough I am fearefull Goddesse of dread warre,
    That hate to liue Idly at home in peace,
With humane cries allured I come from farre,
In streames of bloude to rue this daines decease,
This Lady was a *Howard* and did springe,
Out of the antient Duke of *Norfolkes* race,
Whose ofspring did subdue the *Scots* stout king,
And from the field rebellious foes did chase,
Her brother still restes loyal to the Crowne,
And Scepter which faire *Cynthia* now doth wield,
By Seas he hath obtain'd his high renowne,
The other by his conquest in the field,
    Wherefore I vow by land and Sea to raise,
    Eternall triumphes to the *Howards* praise.

Crowned

QVATORZAIN. 11

Flora.

CRowned with wreathes of Odoriferous flowrs,
Whoſe ſent perfumes the Empire of the *Ayre*,
Among the reſt of the immortall powers,
Vnto the land of *Albion* I repaire.
Where I with garlands will her Toombe adorne,
And make death proud with ceremonious rites,
That for this Ladies ſake I doe not ſcorne, (delights;
To decke her Graue, with th' earths faire flowers
For ſith the world was ſweetned by her breath,
That breath'd rare vertues forth, as then aliue,
Ile beautifie her Sepulcher, ſince death
Of her ſweete ſowle her body did depriue,
  For this braue dame was a ſweet ſpringing flower,
  Bedewde with heauenly grace till her laſt howre.
                                              From

QVATORZAIN. 12.

Proserpina.

FRom the black kingdome of Infernall *Dis*,
All circumſcrib'd with Characters of woe,
And from the dungen of the darke abyſſe,
Wherein the Ocean Seas of troubles flowe,
I doe aſcend vpon this worldly ſtage,
In this ſad Tragedie to act a part,
Sith ſhe that was a light to that laſt age,
Is now confounded by deaths fatall darte;
The cruell deſtinies were much to blame,
To cut her threede of life ere throughly ſpunne,
Her life burnd out like to a *Tapers* flaine,
And thus the howrglaſſe of my ioyes is runne :
  Wherefore the Fatall ſiſters ſhall repent
Her bodies death, and faire ſoules baniſhment.

I

QVATORZAIN. 13.
Aurora.

I now shall blush to kisse the Sunns faire face,
Or bid *bon Iour* vnto this hemyspheare,
I rather will lament in dolefull case,
The losse of her whom I did loue so deare,
I am the Muses euer constant friend
And sith she was their Matrone while she liu'd
I will bewaile for her vntimely ende,
By whom the sacred Sisters were releu'd:
I muse what Muse there is that will not weepe
When *I* shall tell this lamentable story,
That she is dead and now in dust doth sleepe,
Although her soule is crown'd with lasting glory.
   I thinke the world wilbe dissolu'd to teares,
   When this laid tale shall penetrate mens eares.

B   Atty-

QVATORZAIN, 14.
Nox.

Attyrde in black spangled with flames of fier,
Imbroidered with starres in silent night,
While *Phœbus* doth the lower world inspire,
with his bright beames & cōsort breathing spright,
I come in clowds of griefe with pensiue soule,
Sending forth vapours of blacke discontent,
To fill the concaue Circle of the Pole,
And with my teares bedeawe each continent:
Because that she that made my night seeme daye,
By her pure vertues euer shining lamps,
Now makes my night more blacke by her decay,
Wandring with Gholls in the *Elisian* Camps:
  Wherefore I still will were a mourning vaile,
  For she is dead and humane flesh is fraile.

Ad ewe

QVATORZAIN. 15.
Gratia.

ADewe faire *Venus* Ladie of delight,
Welcome pale horror griefe and difcontent,
Come let vs wander to the vaile of night,
And for this Ladies death fighe and lament,
Our hopes late deade ingender liuing feares,
Our griefes awake doe bringe our ioyes afleepe,
Now we from *Thetis* ftreames will borow teares,
And teach the rockes by *Nerleys* fhores to weepe,
Our faire complexion is with forrow chang'd,
We haue bin fellowe Mates with beauties Queene,
But from our felues we now are fo eftrang'd,
We are but fhadowes of what we haue beene,
　　And thus in vaine we daily doe deplore,
　　For loffe of life which we cannot reftore.

QVATORZAIN, 17.
Horaæ.

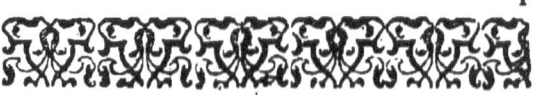

WE that are calde Tymes goldē winged Howres:
And are the Porters of Heauens Chriſtall gate,
Come from the Pallace of Celeſtiall powers,
This Counteſſe death with pompe to celebrate;
By ſhutting vp Heauens gate we ſend downe rayne,
Darking the triple region of the Aire,
And when we liſt opening the doore againe,
Dry the moyſt clowdes & make the weather faire,
Weepe now O clowdes vppon the graſſie earth,
With often drops ſtee through the hardeſt ſtones,
While we in ſorrowe for this Ladies death,
Flie back againe to the Celeſtiall thrones:
    And locking faſt the great Porte of the Skie,
    Send downe more ſhawres for her mortalitie.

I

QVATORZAIN, 18.
Pandora.

I bring a box wherein all woes are clofde,
Mingled with teares diftild from facred eyes,
And not fo much as hope for me repofde
Is left behinde but quite away it flies·
The graces wherewith all the Gods indue me,
Are gone from me and to Ioues throne refort,
The bleffings which vntill this day purfude me,
Forfake me now and I ftand all'amort.
Like *Niobe* that euer till death ftill mourn'de,
For her deare childrens loffe whom *Phoebus* flue,
And to a fenceleffe ftone at laft was turnde,
That in her life did moft extreamely rue:
    And thus transformde I will become a Toombe.
    T'enclofe her vertues in my dying woombe.

If

QVATORZAIN. 18.

Pales Dea pastorum.

IF kingdomes waile shall not the Cottage weepe?
  If the Court greeue shall not the Country grone?
If they doe morne that doe strong Lions keepe?
Shall not I, that keepe tender sheepe, bemoue?
If faire *Elisa* monarch of this Ile,
This Ladies losse doth gratiously lament,
It ill becomes a country swayne to smyle,
Or me that ann the Shepheards presidence:
O thou rare Queene that makest the femal gender,
By much, more worthie then the Masculine,
To thee all praise and glorie I surrender,
Whom I esteeme as sacred and deuine;
    Had not thy life giuen shepheards sweet releese,
    I should haue well nigh perished with greefe.
Euen

·QVATORZAIN, 19.
Feronia.

EVen in this ſad and melancholy moode,
With *Siluan Nimphes* which on me daily tende
Mated with ſorrowe come I from the woode,
And to faire *Cynthias* kingdome now I wende,
Where the immortall Goddeſſes arriu'd,
At *Troynouant*, by which *Thames* waues do glide,
Where late a Ladie of great honour liu'd,
But greater vertue, that vntimely dyde:
Thither goe I among the reſt to mourne,
And offer vp my teares vpon her ſhrine,
My loftie trees I will cut downe and burne,
In wittneſſe of her death for which I pyne:
  And as my trees conſume away with flame
   So doth my heart with griefe, and ioy with ſhame.

In

QVATORZAIN. 15.
Libitina.

IN dreary accents of a dolefull verse,
Ile speake her praise though I haue long bin dübe,
In sable weedes ile decke her dismall hearse,
And sacrifice my tears vpon her toombe;
With golden Statues shall her toombe be gilte,
Like King *Mansolus* stately monument,
Which his deare wife the *Queene* of *Caria* built
To be the worldes eternall wonderment.
Or else I will her sencelesse corps interre,
In some faire graue like the *Pyramides*,
And will enbalme her bodie with sweete Mirrh
With *Cassia*, *Ambergreece* and *Aloes*   (smell,
  That th'Ayre perfum'd therewith shall sweetly
  While heauenly powers shal ring her wofull knel.
                                        An-

 *Erecinthia* alias *Rhea Cybele Ops Ve-*
sta, Tellus, &c. as *Hesiodus* saith was
the daughter of *Cælum* and *Terra* the
wife of *Saturne*, commonly called the
mother of the gods & goddesses of the
earth ; whome Poets faine to be drawne by foure
Lions in a chariot with a crowne of Towres on her
head and a royall scepter in her hand, she is also re-
puted the founder of Cities and Towres for defence.

Iuno called *Pronuba* and of some *Lucina* the
daughter of *Saturne* and *Ops*, wife and sister of *Iupi-*
ter, Queene of heauen, and goddesse of riches, im-
palled with the celestiall diademe, drawne in her
chariot by Peacockes, she is accounted to predomi-
nate mariages, and the birth of children.

Pallas otherwise called *Minerua* as *Hesiodus* affirmeth is the daughter of *Neptune* and *Triton*, poetically

tically alſo fayned to be engendred of the braine of
Jupiter : She is the Goddeſſe of wiſedome, learning,
and the liberall ſciences , She is the ſiſter of *Mars*
and is ſaid to be the Goddeſſe of warres and martiall
ſtratagems , and for that is often called *Bellona.*

Cynthia called alſo *Diana* and *Phœbe* the daughter
of *Iupiter* and *Latona* the ſiſter of *Phœbus* ſhe is the
Goddeſſe of hunting and fiſhing, who addicting her
ſelfe wholy to virginitie obtained of *Iupiter* therefore to liue in the woods. *Virgil. Lib. 11. Alme tibi hāc
nemorum cultrix Latonia virgo.*

Venus termed alſo *Cytherea* poetically fained to
be bred of the froth of the Sea, excelled all other
Goddeſſes in beautie , ſhe is the Goddeſſe of loue,
pleaſures and laſciuious delightes, ſhe rideth in a chariot drawne by doues, ſhe is the mother of *Cupid* and
is accounted one of the ſeuen planets

Thetis

Thetis called also *Amphitrite* the wife of *Peleus* King of *Theffalie*, daughter of *Nereus* and mother of *Achilles* was efteemed Goddeffe of the Sea: of *Nereus* all the Nymphes were called *Nereides.*

Ceres the daughter of *Saturne* and *Ops* fifter of *Iupiter* & *Pluto*, is the Goddeffe of Corne drawen in her chariot by dragons, crownde with fheaues of wheat fhe wandred about the world to finde her daughter *Proferpina* whom *Pluto* ftole away, fhe firft taught the vfe of the plough and to till the land.

Aurora the morning, the daughter of *Hyperion* and *Thia* in the iudgement of *Hefiodus*, or as others fay of *Titan* and *Terra* whom for her faire vermilion colour *Homer* faineth to haue fingers of damaske rofes, and to be drawne by bright bay horfes in a golden charriot, fhe is faid by *Orpheus* not only to be a moft comforrable Ladie to men, but alfo to beafts and plants and is a great friend to the Mufes.

Nox

Nox the night, bred of *Chaos* as Poets faine whom they cal the most auntient mother of all creatures, because there was no light but darkenes before the Sunne and the heauens were made. And she possessed all places before the birth of the gods, she is cloathed in blacke rayment, with a sable vayle vpon her head, transported by blacke horses in her eben chariot, she came from *Erebus* and the infernals obscuring this Hemysphere when the Sunne is gone to the *Antipodes.*

Flora called also *Chloris* the wife of *Zephirus* is deemed the goddesse of Flowres:

Bellona the goddesse of warre called also *Pallas,* which to expresse both the valour and the wisedome of the honorable race of the *Howardes* I haue twise expressed in seuerall sonnets, whom *Virgil* nameth the president of warre.

A·mi-

Armipotens belli præses Tritonia Pallas

Fortuna as some suppose vvas the daughter of *Oceanus*, albeit *Hesiodus* writing of the originall birth of the Gods, makes no mention of her , yet she is vainely reckoned among the number of the Gods as *Iuuenal* witnesseth.

> *Nullum numen abest si sit prudentia, sed te*
> *Nos facimus Fortuna deam Cæloq́, locamus.*

She is the Goddesse of chance and inconstancie she is saide to be blinde and to be rouled about vpon a wheale as *Tibullus* in 1. *Elegiarum*. *Versatur celeri Fors leuis orbe rota.*

Proserpina called also *Persephone* and of some *Hecate* is the daughter of *Iupiter* and *Ceres*, the wife of *Pluto* Queene of Hell, she hath souraigne power of dead bodies.

Nemesis

Nemesis the daughter of *Oceanus* and *Nox* may be called the Goddesse of reuenge, who was sent from *Iupiter* to suppresse the pride and insolence of such as are to much puft vp with arrogancie for the fruitio of worldly felicitie: and therfore *Aristotle Li.de muni de*, affirmeth *Nemesis* to be the deuine power and iustice of God to punish malefactors for their haynous crimes, and to distribute to euery one accor-ding to his demerits.

Libitina is the Goddesse of Funeralls.

The Graces called *Gratiæ* or *Charites* the Graces daughters of *Iupiter* and *Eurynome* whose names are *Aglaia, Euphrosyne* and *Thalia*, they were beautifull and the companions of *Venus*.

Hore the howres, daughters of *Iupiter* and *Themis*, are by *Homer* and other Poets saide to keepe the gates of heauen, and by opening of them to make faire weather, and by shutting them to make foule weather

weather, they fauour learning and associate *Venus*
and the Graces: They are imagined to haue soft feet
and to be most slow of all the Goddesses, and still to
worke some new matter, they moderate and de-
uide the succession of times,

Pandora, a Ladie imbellished with all fayre ornaments of bodie and minde on whome euery one of
the Gods bestowed a seuerall gift of grace, was sent
by *Ioue* to *Prometheus* with all euils inclosed, sait in a
box or little cofer, which gift being refused by *Prometheus* was by her brought to *Epimetheus*, who o-
pening the couer of the box, perceiuing all those e-
uils to flie out suddenly shut the same, reseruing only
hope in the bottome thereof reposed which he kept
fast; which hope you must imagine now that *Pandora* hath lost in the cariage by reason of this most
noble Countesse death.

Niobe

Niobe the daughter of *Tantalus* waxing infolent beyond meafure for the beautie and goodly propor-tion of her children, infomuch that fhe compared or rather preferred her felfe in opinion of glory before *Latona* and her facred ofspring was therefore by the decree of the Gods metamorphofed into a ftone, and fo became her owne bodies fepulcher; and her children were flaine by *Phœbus* and *Diana* with ar-rowes as Poets fayne.

Pales is the Goddeffe of Shepheards in honour of whofe diety Shepheards did celebrate certain games called *Palilia.*

. *Feronia* the Goddeffe of woods or groues whofe temple (as *Strabo* writeth) was famous in the Citie *Soractes*, and fhe with great deuotion was there wor-fhipped, of whome there is no mention made touch-ing her birth or education, notwithftanding fhe is rec koned foueraigne of the woods as *Virgil* writeth,

    Et viridi gaudens Feronia luco.   Great

QVATORZIAN. 1
Clio.

GReat princes actes I vſe to royalize,
  And from the Stigian ſtouds their fame to ſaue,
And in the Criſtall mirror of the skies,
With wits faire Diamond I their praiſe ingraue:
By me *Alcmenas* ſonne is made deuine,
And faire *Caliſto* turned to a Beare
Now in the Starrie firmament doth ſhine,
And with her light adornes this Hemyſphere,
And I will raiſe to heauen this hoble dame,
Aboue the pureſt Element of fire,
And lo in Starres charaꝪerize hir fame;
That time ſhall not her glories date expire,
    And yet my heart in pittie takes remorſe,
    For her deare ſoule and bodies late diuorſe.

C   Knowing

QVATORZIAN. 2

Melpomene.

KNowing her life what shall I sound her praise?
Or musing of her death fall in a sounde?
Shall I recorde her fame in my sweete laies?
Or by my sorrow make her death renownde?
I know not what to doe, I am amazde,
I wander in a Laborinth of woes,
Her praise alreadie through the world is blazd,
And now her death with greefe I must disclose;
Wherefore I register her death with teares,
Which doe turne blacke with sorrowe in the fall,
Wringing my handes renting my golden heares,
And with these reliques grace her funerall,
　　Exclaming thus with euerlasting cries,
　　Vertue grows sicke, shame liues, true honor dies.

I

QVATORZAIN. 3
Thalia.

I That in Princes Pallaces was bred,
And did delight in euerie comicke sport,
Whose daintie feete on carpets vsde to treade,
And dance the measures statly in the courr,
Will turne my mirthfull songs to dolefull cries,
And fill with teares the *Heliconian* brooke,
My louely cheekes besmeard withweeping eyes,
Like fleshlesse deathes Anatomie I looke,
For she that brought new reuels out of *France*,
When she returned to her natiue soyle,
Who sought my glory chiefly to aduance,
Hath now by death receiued a fatall foile,
    Thus by herlosse I am compeld to rue
    That she to soone hath bid the world adewe.

             C 2   Come

QVATORZAIN. 4

Euterpe.

COme sisters let vs sing sad roundelaies,
  And stréw green Cypres boughs vpō hir Tombe
Crowning her image with immortall bayes,
Oh sacred ofspring of *Latonas* wombe,
Play on thy seauen-strunge harpe and sadly warble,
The wailefull murmur of celestiall spheares,
And while thou doest engraue her fame in marble,
Ile digge her greue with showres of sacred teares;
My pipe shall make the stones to weepe for pitte,
As great *Amphions* Lyre did make them dance,
To build againe the ruynes of that Citie,
Which did maintaine the Grecian puisance,
    And yet not *Thebes* but *Troynouant* shall mourne
    For her whose flesh to Elements did turne.

What

QVATORZAIN. 5
Terpsichore.

VVHat dolefull *Diapason* shall I make,
  What mournfull songs of sorrow shall I sing
What comfort in sweete Musicke can I take,
Sith death hath broke this Ladies vitall string:
My sacred Lyre that did resound of yore,
Celestiall harmony, like *Phœbus* Lute,
Such ioyfull accents now shall sound no more,
For inward sorrow makes our consort mute;
Sith death hath broke that string that did vnite
In mutuall loue her bodie and her soule,
My dulcimers shall make no more delight
And I will liue in euerlasting dole
    For how can Musicke solace humaine eares,
    Whē strings are broke & harts are drownd in tears

C 3   Ye

QVATORZAIN. 6.
Erato.

YE that like *Iulius Cæsar* seeke to measure,
  The spacious clymates of the centred round,
To fish for kingdomes and to purchase treasure,
Oppose your liues to euerie fatall wound,
Behold euen in the map of my sad face,
A true Cosmographie of humane woes,
For since foule death his Trophees heare did place,
In quiet rest I neuer could repose,
Vnto th'Antarticke Pole what need ye saile,
At home in safetie better may yee sleepe,
Consider by her death your flesh is fraile,
Sit downe by me vppon these rockes and weepe,
    For *Albion* now more sorrowes doth containe,
    Then there is wealth in all the Ocean mayne.
                                        Were

QVATORZAIN. 7
Calliope.

VVEre it nor that *Eliza* did reuiue,
  My drooping spirits that are like to perish,
If that worlds myrrour onely she aliue,
Did not with bountie still my Poems cherish,
I should goe languish in some obscure caue,
Or with rude Satyres, & wood-nymphs should dwel
Learning should lie in base *Obliuions* graue,
And flow no more from *Aganippe* well:
But since this Ladies soule is vanished,
Out of this world (her corps to death enthrald)
She to a starre is metamorphosed
And with the golden Twinns in heauen enstald
    Or like the *Pleiades* enthron'd on high
    She may be term'd a *Phœnix* in the skie.

C 4   I saw

QVATORZAIN. 8.

Vrania.

I Sawe no fearefull comet in the Skye,
Nor firie Meteors lately did I viewe,
Whose dread aspect threatens mortalitie,
And losse of some great Princes to insue:
Nor by Astrologie did I deuine,
That death so soone this Paragon should slay,
That she who did in grace and vertue shine,
Aboue her Peeres before them should decay,
I thinke while all the Gods in counsell sate,
To canonize some Saint, that late did die,
Not being mindfull of this Ladies state,
Whose fatall howre did then approach so nigh,
  Death stole vppon her with his *Eben* darte
  And vnwares did strike her to the heart.

Sith

QVATORZAIN. 9.
Polyhymnia.

SIth I am tearm'd the Muses Oratrix,
My pen shall wright the Iliades of my greefe,
My tearefull eyes vppon her beare ile fixe,
My tongue shall tell a wofull tale in breefe:
My hands shall act the passions of my minde,
My ruthfull lookes bewray my pensiue thought,
I will complaine the Fates are too vnkinde,
Frō bad to worse the world still growes to nought:
Wherefore I thinke that *Plato's* wondrous yeare,
(When as the Orbs of Heauen shalbe reuolu'd,
To their first course) approcheth very neare
The bands of th' Elements shalbe dissolu'd:
    And till those daies of consummation come,
    Cares make me passionate & sorrowes dombe.
                      Now

NOw *Goddesses* and *Muses* giue me leaue,
In this sad Tragedie to acte a part,
I haue more cause for her decease to greeue,
Though you more wit to shew your sorrows smart:
Yee for affection doe extoll her praise,
And for mere pittie doe her death lament,
I both for loue and duetie striue to raise
Her fame aboue the starrie firmament:
And death for enuie did abridge her daies
T'enritch his kingdome with this vertuous dame
But I for griefe that death the Tyrant plaies,
Impouerisht haue my wit t'enrich her fame
  While I performe these rites which are most fit,
  Death waxeth rich in spoyle, I spoild of witte.
                                        An.

THE nine *Muses* which are the presidents of Poets and first authors of Poetry Musicke & other sciences, are the daughters of *Iupiter* & *mnemosyne alias memoria* whose names are *Clio*, *Melpomine*, *Thalia*, *Eutepre*, *Terpsichore*, *Erato*, *Calliope*, *Vrania* & *Polihimnia*. *Clio* exerciseth her wit & skill chiefely in Histories and recording the actes & monuméts of worthie persons, *Melpomine* in Tragedies, and lamentable *Elegies*, *Thalia* in Comedies, comely gestures, and sweete speeches, *Euterpe* in the pipe & such like instruments, *Terpsichore* in the Citterne or Lute, *Erato* in Geometrie, or Chosmographie, *Calliope* in heroicke verses, *Vrania* in Astrologie and contemplation of the starres, and *Polihimnia* in Rhetorick and Eloquence.

De-

Deuine sonnets dedicated to the said Lady not
long before her decease by the said Author.

Of Gods holy name, Iehouah, or Tetragrammaton.

THat name which *Moses* on his forehead bare,
   I in my heart doe worship and adore,
That name which Iewes to name did seldome dare,
May I presume for mercie to implore?
That name which *Salomon* vppon his breast,
*I*n his diuine Pentaculum did weare,
With great *Iehouah* Characters imprest,
That name I loue I reuerence and feare:
That name which *Aron* wore vpon his head,
Grau'd in his holy *Miter* made of Golde,
That name which Angels laude and furies dreade,
Whose praise no tongue can worthily vnfolde,
   That name which flesh is to impure to name,
My sinfull soule with sacred zeale inflame.

Of

Of the Starre which the Magi did worſhip at
Chriſtes Natiuitie, and of his death.

I blaze that ſtarre, which was no blazing ſtarre,
  But the true figure of eternall life,
The prince of peace was borne then ceaſed warre,
His birthes beginning ended mortall ſtrife,
This glorious ſtarre did lead the aged wiſe
To worſhip th'*Infants* Godhead in the Eaſt,
Which came with gladſome heart & ioyfull eyes,
To ſee that Babe that made all *Iſraell* bleſt:
O light of Heauen thou waſt extinct on earth,
Yet to our ſoules Celeſtiall life doth giue
Thy death our life, thy riſing our new birth
Thou three daies dead didſt make vs euer liue,
  Yet at thy death obſcur'd was th'earth and ſkie,
  Becauſe he that was God, as man did die.

Foun-

FOuntaine of grace from whom doth only runne;
Water of life to faue our foules from death,
O fauiour of the world, pure virgins fonne,
That in red earth infuf'd firft vitall breath.
Oh thou whofe name was calde *Emmanuel*,
Ioyning thy Godhead with humanitie,
Thou that for our fakes didft defcend to hell,
And ouer death did'ft get the victorie:
Oh womans feede that didft from God proceede,
By Prophets faid to breake the Serpents head,
Thou that in grace and vertue doeft exceede,
Content to die that thou mighteft quicken deade,
   Thou that didft rayfe the dead men frô the tombe.
Earths kingdoms paffe, oh let thy kingdome come.
                          Antient

A Ntient of daies, and yet ſtill young in yeares,
Oh *God* on earthe, Oh man yet moſt deuine,
Poore in this world, yet chiefe of heauenly Peeres,
Whoſe glorie in th'infernall pit did ſhine,
Borne ſince old *Abrahams* daies yet long before,
(For *Abraham* reioyc'd to ſee thy daies)
He ſaw by faith, whom now all powers adore,
The *Cerubins* doe daily ſing thy praiſe,
O *God* oftymes, and yet in time a man,
Before all times thy time of being was,
And yet in time thy humaine birth beganne,
Leaſt we ſhould fade vntimely like the graſſe,
  Oh thou that doeſt all times beginne and ende,
  Graunt all our workes may to thy glory tende,

Of

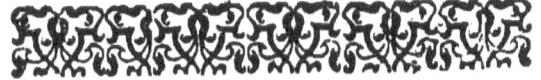

VVHere liues the man that neuer felt a croſſe?
Who Fortunes wheel did neuer tumble down
Where liues the man that neuer ſuffred loſſe ?
On whome the ſtarres of heauen did neuer frowne ?
Where liues the man that is in all poln tes bleſt?
Wiſe valiant, mightie, wealthy, fayre and ſtrong,
If ſuch a one vpon the earth doth reſt
His date of life Heauen doth abridge ere long
Such was King *Edward* in his youthfull prime
Who might by *Phæbus* Oracle be deemd
One of the wiſeſt Princes of his time
For wit and learning excellent eſteemde
But cruell death maligning his great praiſe
That in ſewe yeares ſo highly did aſpyre
With yron dart inſtring'd his golden daies
Whom nations farre away did then admyre
Weeds long time growe, the ſayreſt flowres do fade
The ripeſt wits grow rotten at the laſt
All theſe faire things which God and Nature made
In

In this huge *Chaos*, shall at length lye waste
Where is king *Salomon* the wisest wight
Of mortall men that liu'd vpon the grounde
Doth he not wander in the shades of night,
Whose wisdome through the world was forenound?
What difference betwixt the rich and poore
Irus with *Cresus* boldly may compare
Both equall are when death standes at the doore
That maketh proudest kings like beggars bare,
Then let the wealthy men respect their end
Not couuting themselues happy vntyll death,
Sith heauen to them this wealth doth only lende,
Which they must pay with losse of vitall breath
This made that king of *Lidia* to crye
When he was by king *Cyrus* ouercome:
O *Solon* now thy saying true I trie
No man is happie till his day of dome.
That Monarch now is dead that did possesse,
The golden sands of bright *Pactolus* waues,
And *Tambertaine* whom Fortune so did blesse,

D

That

That he a Shepheard made great kings his slaues,
Dead is that mightie king of *Macedon*,
That wept whe of more worlds he hard some talke,
Sith his victorious sword as then had wonne,
Scarce this one world, where we like pilgrims walk
Who being wounded fell vpon one knee,
Fighting against an hoast of barbarous foes,
Said I am mortall by these wounds I see,
For no such bloode from powers Celestiall flowes.
In beautie *Absalon* did farre excell,
Most part of men that sprung of humaine seede,
But when against his Sire he did rebell, (head:
Then heauen did power downe vengeance on his
The sacred scripture truely doth expresse,
That *Sampson* did surpasse all men in strength,
But he that did thowsands in fight distresse,
Was by a womans wiles subdu'd at length,
Beautie is like a faire but fading flower,
Riches are like a bubble in a streame,
Great strength is like a fortefied Towre.

Hono:

Honour is like a vaine but pleaſing dreame,
Wee ſee the fayreſt flowers ſoone fade away,
Bubbles doe quickly vaniſh like the winde,
Strong Towers are rent, and doe in tyme decay,
And dreames are but illuſions of the minde,
Let none puſt vp with inſolence deride,
My Fortunes *Autumne* in my prime of yeares,
Sith many diſmall chances do betide,
To royall princes and State-ruling peeres,
I am content with my diſaſter chance,
To follow fate ſith princes lead the daunce,

Ludit in Humanis diuina potentia rebus.
Et certam praſens vix habet hora fidem.

D 3

FVNERALL
LAMENTACIONS
VPON THE DEATH OF

his moſt worthy and reuerend vnckle
Maiſter MATHEW EWENS Eſquire one
of her Maieſties Barons of her High-
nes Court of Eſchequer.

***

LONDON,
Printed by RICHARD BRADOCKE
for I B. 1598.

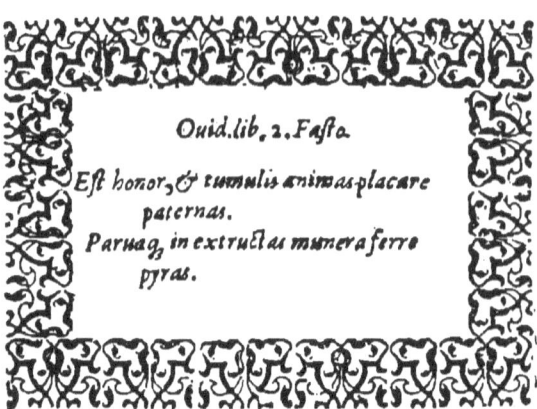

Ouid. lib. 2. Fasto.

Est honor, & tumulis animas placare
    paternas.
Paruaq, in extructas munera ferre
    pyras.

L E T *Numas* death be ſtill deplorde in Rome,
  Licurgus end let famous *Sparta* waile,
  Let *Athens* weepe on *Ariſtides* toombe,
  For there religion lawes and Iuſtice faile,
But let faire *Cinthias Tropuonant* lament,
This Barons death whoſe fleſh returnes to duſt,
Whoſe ſoule is fled aboue the firmament,
Who liu'd on earth religious, true, and iuſt.
Now i oye O heauen t'enioy th'earths ornament,
Whoſe heauenly part to the third heauen is fled
His earthly part to earth doth now relent
Both heauen and earth loue him aliue and dead,
  His fleſh to Elements reſolu'd doth dye,
  His ſoule aboue the Element doth flye.

D 4

I

QVATORZAIN. 2.

I Know not whether I fhould icy or weepe
His louing foule doth triumph in the fkie,
But his dead corps in dult a while doth fleepe,
Till heauen fhall rayfe it from mortalitie,
He loft his olde life and hath gaind a newe
Loofing nis care he gainde a glorious crowne,
The world loft him, therefore the world doth rue,
He loft the world yet wins for aye renowne,
I loft a friende and therefore I lament,
My friend loft me and I haue loft my felfe
Sith I for his loffe liue in difcontent
He loues heauens ioyes and leaues all worldly pelfe,
  O England now bewaile thisfatall croffe,
He loft this world , we gainde a world of loffe.
He

QVATORZAIN. 3

HE that did feeke the poore mens wrongs to right
 He that maintain'd his natiue countries lawes,
He that in trueth and iuftice did delight
Is now confum'd by deaths deuouring iawes,
Was it by heauens high court of Parliament,
Decreed that his lifes date fo foone fhould ende,
Oh then let vs vpon the earth lament
That we haue loft in him a publique friend
The ioy of many in his graue now lieth,
And he in heauen enioyes immortall bliffe,
His care is vaniſht and in him now dieth,
And liues in others that his life doe miffe
   Thus death ſtrooke many with this fatall ſtroke
   And keeping natures lawes, our lawes He broke.

Let

QVATORZAIN. 4.

LEt not the world thinke I doe partialize,
  In that I doe extoll my vncles fame,
And striue his glorie to immortalize
By these sad accents which my muse doth frame,
But let men know that he deserues more praise,
Then my poore muse is able to bestow,
Though she doth crown his death with glorious baies
And through the world the breath of fame doth blow
Which breath by multiplying the sweete ayre
May mount the sacred Throne of heauenly powers,
And cause the winged Cherubins repayre,
To mourne his death from their celestiall bowres,
    His vertues merit *Homers* golden pen
    To print his praise with teares of Gods and men.
            Let

QVATORZAIN.

Let all men iudge how iuſt a Iudge he was,
 That late was iudged by heauen ſacred doome,
To ſuffer death, that when this life ſhould paſſe
He might obtaine in heauen a glorious roome,
For he among the bleſſed ſaints muſt dwell
Where Patriarches and the Apoſtles ſit,
Which ſhall iudge the twelue Tribes of Iſrael
According as to their deſerts is fit
As here on earth this Iudge was magnifide
Aboue the vulgar ſort in high degree,
In heauen he ſhalbe much more gloꝛifide,
And ſhall enioy the full felicitie,
    And all ſuch Iudges as here iudge aright,
    Shall haue their place in heaué with Angels bright.
                                        The

QVATORZAIN. 6

'THe sacred word doth say thou shalt not kill
  Yet Death thou here doest kill a magistrate ;
Dost thou not then infringe Gods holy will
Nor yet the lawes of *Moses* violate?
And wheras mightie kings establish lawes
Thou by thine owne lawe mighty Kings doest slay,
And taking thus away th'efficient cause,
'Th'effect, which is the Lawe must needs decay,
Thus now thou takest away a publique guide,
That did maintaine all equitie and right.
Wherefore heauen shall correct thee for thy pride
And shall subdue thy all-flesh-killing might,
    And thou that dost all creatures ouercome,
    Shalt be at last destroyed by heauens iust doome.
                                                    If

QVATORZAIN. 7

IF that the foule (as fome fuppofed) might goe,
Out of one bodie to an others breſt,
Would that meeke ſpirit which from him did flow,
In euery Lawyers heart were now impreſt
His lifes integritie and zeale was ſuch
He more eſteemd of honeſtie then gold
Which in any now a daies doe loue too much
For loue is oft with money bought and ſold,
This rightly may be termde a golden age,
With gold. is fame and reputation bought
Yet *Salomon* that was moſt wiſe and ſage,
For wiſedome praide, eſteeming gold as nought.
Gold vnto droſſe and fleſh to duſt muſt turne,
For this mans loſſe let the Eſchequer mourne.

Aurea mire verè ſunt ſecula o͡u͡r imus amor.
Venit bonos, auro conciliatur amor.

¶ In obitum Patrui sui colendissimi
Mathei Eueni *illustrissimi Baronis*
Scaccarij *T. R.* nepotis Nænia, siue
carmen funebre.

Tristia Melpomine lachrymarum flumina funde,
    Sit cum perpetuo iunctus amore dolor.
Ille pater patrie pollens pietate, Patronus
    Pauperis, & Plebis, per mala fata perit,
Spritus ascendit splendentis culmen Olympi,
    Diuitias cœli, quas cupiebat, habet.
Non rapuit fiscus, quod non vult Christus habere.
    Non plus quam licuit conciliauit opes.
Ille mihi Patruus charus, patriáq, patriq,
    Ergo suus deflet funera mesta nepos.
Doctus erat, facilis natura, mente benignus,
    Moribus humanus, deniq, morte pius:
Lege Solon, grauitate Cato, sed Tullius ore,
    Nestor consilijs, & pietate Plato.
Membra tegit tumulus, viuit post funera fœlix,
    Fama viget mundo, spiritus astra colit.
Purpureos spargam flores, opobalsama fundam,
    Et plenis manibus lilia pulchra dabo.
His, altem exequijs & munere fungar inani,
    Hic animam denis accumulare velim.

Non

Non grates expecto tamen, nec proemia curo,
  Non hominum laudes: hoc pietatis opus.
Cogit amor patriæ patriæ lugere parentem
  Defunctam, tantò debitus urget honos.
O decus, O patriæ nuper lux, atq, columna
  Natalisq, soli gloria magna vale.
O longum venerande vale, vale. inquit Eucne
  Qui tuus est semper fidus amansque Nepos,
Sic vivam & moriar semper tibi certus amicus,
  Musaque cum fatis est moriturus tuis
Iurisconsultus, naturæ iure peremptus
  Nunc stabit æterni Iudicis ante Thronum
Qui, vnios homines diuino iudicet ore,
  Iudex istius Iudicis almus erit.
Sic piâ vita fuit, nunc terq; quaterq; beata,
  In rutilo vivit, nobilis umbra Polo.

F I N I S.